Welcome to ALADDIN QUIX!

If you are looking for fast, fun-to-read stories
with colorful characters, lots of kid-friendly
humor, easy-to-follow action, entertaining
story lines, and lively illustrations, then
ALADDIN QUIX is for you!

But wait, there's more!

If you're also looking for stories with
tables of contents; word lists; about-the-
book questions; 64, 80, or 96 pages; short
chapters; short paragraphs; and large fonts,
then **ALADDIN QUIX** is *definitely* for you!

ALADDIN QUIX: The next step between ready
to reads and longer, more challenging chapter
books, for readers five to eight years old.

Read all the ALADDIN QUIX books!

By Stephanie Calmenson

Our Principal Is a Frog!
Our Principal Is a Wolf!
Our Principal's in His Underwear!
Our Principal Breaks a Spell!

Royal Sweets
By Helen Perelman

Book 1: *A Royal Rescue*
Book 2: *Sugar Secrets*
Book 3: *Stolen Jewels*

A Miss Mallard Mystery
By Robert Quackenbush

Dig to Disaster
Texas Trail to Calamity
Express Train to Trouble
Stairway to Doom
Bicycle to Treachery
Gondola to Danger
Surfboard to Peril
Taxi to Intrigue

Little Goddess Girls
By Joan Holub and Suzanne Williams

Book 1: *Athena & the Magic Land*

A Miss Mallard Mystery

SURFBOARD TO PERIL

ROBERT QUACKENBUSH

ALADDIN QUIX

New York   London   Toronto   Sydney   New Delhi

ALADDIN QUIX
Simon & Schuster Children's Publishing Division
1230 Avenue of the Americas, New York, New York 10020
This Aladdin QUIX paperback edition May 2019
Copyright © 1986 by Robert Quackenbush
Also available in an Aladdin QUIX hardcover edition.
All rights reserved, including the right of reproduction in whole or in part in any form.
ALADDIN and the related marks and colophon are trademarks of Simon & Schuster, Inc.
For information about special discounts for bulk purchases, please contact
Simon & Schuster Special Sales at 1-866-506-1949 or business@simonandschuster.com.
The Simon & Schuster Speakers Bureau can bring authors to your live event. For
more information or to book an event contact the Simon & Schuster Speakers Bureau
at 1-866-248-3049 or visit our website at www.simonspeakers.com.
Designed by Tiara Iandiorio
The illustrations for this book were rendered in pen and ink and wash.
The text of this book was set in Archer Medium.
Manufactured in the United States of America 0720 OFF
2 4 6 8 10 9 7 5 3
Library of Congress Control Number 2018959535
ISBN 978-1-5344-1418-1 (hc)
ISBN 978-1-5344-1417-4 (pbk)
ISBN 978-1-5344-1419-8 (eBook)

First for Piet and Margie,

and now for Emma and Aidan

Cast of Characters

Miss Mallard: World-famous ducktective

Kai and Kawai: Two surfers who taught Miss Mallard how to surf

Clyde Pochard: A builder

Good King Kalakaua: Ancient ancestor of Kai and Kawai

Horace Shoveller: Scientist who digs for ancient Hawaiian art

Joe Scaup: Old sailor who combs the beach for junk to sell

What's in
Miss Mallard's Bag?

Miss Mallard has many detective tools she brings with her on her adventures around the world.

In her knitting bag she usually has:

- Newspaper clippings
- Knitting needles and yarn
- A magnifying glass
- A flashlight
- A mirror
- A travel guide
- Chocolates for her nephew

Contents

Chapter 1: Surf's Up!   1

Chapter 2: Friendly Feast 13

Chapter 3: Missing Stone 22

Chapter 4: On the Run! 32

Chapter 5: Special Delivery 38

Chapter 6: The Jig Is Up! 48

Word List   62

Questions   65

Acknowledgments 67

1

Surf's Up!

While surfing in Hawaii, the world-famous ducktective **Miss Mallard** hit a large stone with her surfboard.

Whomp!

She was tossed hard on the

sand and just missed being run over by a bulldozer.

"Watch where you're going!" yelled the driver as he raced by without stopping.

Two young Hawaiian surfers who were gathering fresh coconuts from nearby palm trees saw the trouble and came running. Their names were **Kai and Kawai**. They had taught Miss Mallard how to surf.

"Are you okay, Miss Mallard?" asked Kai.

"Just a bit shaken," replied Miss Mallard, pointing to the waves. "My surfboard hit that large stone. But I'm wondering why the driver of that bulldozer didn't stop."

"That's **Clyde Pochard** for you," said Kawai. "He's a builder. He only thinks of himself and his condominiums. He is the reason Kai's family and my family are bitter enemies."

Kawai took a deep breath and continued. "He wants my family

to sell the beachfront property between our two villages. Kai's family says my family has no right to sell because the land is also theirs."

"Oh my!" said Miss Mallard.

"However," Kawai explained, "my family has an old chart that says the land is ours. That is what the **feud** is all about. Still, it hasn't kept Kai and me from being friends just because our families don't get along."

While Kawai and Miss Mallard

were talking, Kai went to have a look at the stone Miss Mallard hit with her surfboard.

"Kawai!" he shouted. **"Come have a look!"**

Kawai ran to Kai, and the two friends began jumping up and down with excitement. Then they dragged the stone from the shallow water and brought it to shore.

Miss Mallard saw that the stone was carved with ancient signs and symbols.

"What is it?" she asked, puzzled.

"This is the sacred stone of our ancestors," said Kawai. "Legends say that our ancient ancestor **Good King Kalakaua** placed it on a pedestal on the very land I told you about." Kawai paused.

"Then a great **tidal wave** came and swept it away, leaving an empty pedestal that still stands," he explained, pointing across the beach.

"The stone is older than my family's chart. It proves *both* our families own the land," he said.

"Lucky for us, a wave brought it back after all this time, and you found it, Miss Mallard," said Kai.

"We must tell our families the news and replace the stone on its pedestal. From now on, neither family will be able to sell the land without consent of the other family."

Miss Mallard, Kai, and Kawai all went together to the pedestal. Kai and Kawai placed the stone in its rightful place.

Then Kai picked up a **conch** shell from the sand and blew into it.

"Aaaaawoooooooo!"

"What a useful shell!" said Miss Mallard. "I found one like it on the beach today. I may use it to call taxis whenever I go shopping in London, which is outside my home in the English countryside."

2

Friendly Feast

Kawai blew the conch again, and all up and down the beach, folks came running. They gathered around the pedestal.

The leaders of the two villages stepped forward, and when they saw the stone, they were ashamed. They were reminded of their heritage and the ancestor they all shared, Good King Huminhamin. They were sorry they had quarreled, and they made peace.

"We must promise never to sell the land," said the leader of Kai's village. "We shall keep it for future generations."

"Agreed," said the leader of Kawai's village. "Now let's have a feast."

"Hooray!" everyone shouted.

While the villagers gathered to prepare for the **luau**, the news about the recovery of the legendary stone spread far and wide.

Clyde Pochard was the first to hear the news, and he raced down to the beach—*zoom*—in his bulldozer.

Everyone could see that he was furious because he had lost his chance to buy the land.

He honked his horn—*beep*—and splattered the villagers with sand as he went by.

Then came two nosy ducks who were pestering everyone to have a look at the stone.

One was **Horace Shoveller**, a scientist who digs for ancient Hawaiian art pieces. The other was **Joe Scaup**, an old sailor who combs the beach for junk he sells to tourists. They were promptly chased away.

At last the celebration began. A band played while dancers wearing flowing grass skirts did the **hula**. Miss Mallard was invited to dance with the others. She quickly caught on to the steps and movements as though she had been wearing a grass skirt all her life.

Everyone danced until the sun set, and then they all sat down to a marvelous feast of pineapple, **poi**, and many other Hawaiian specialties.

All during the feasting, Miss Mallard was toasted often for finding the treasured ancestral stone.

"Here's to our hero! Cheers to Miss Mallard!" everyone said as they held up their cups in **unison**.

After the feast everyone lit candles and gathered around the stone to sing good-night songs. They hummed all the way to the pedestal. But when they got there, their hums changed to yells of horror.

The stone was not there!

3

Missing Stone

"Call the police!" someone cried.

"No!" said the leader of Kai's village. "The police would never believe a story about a legendary stone that was found, then lost again—all in a single day."

"I agree," said the leader of Kawai's village. "We would all look foolish."

Miss Mallard stepped forward with her knitting bag that contained her detective kit.

"I'll investigate this case," she said.

Everyone stepped aside, and Miss Mallard set to work. First she dusted the pedestal's base and looked for featherprints. There were none. Then she looked all around for fingerprints. They had all been brushed away. Then she examined the top of the pedestal where the stone had rested.

She saw a clue! It was a key chain with a carving of a scary face dangling from it. It was carved from a shark's tooth.

Miss Mallard aimed a flashlight at the strange key chain.

"Does anyone recognize this?" she asked.

All was quiet. Everyone shook their heads.

"So," said Miss Mallard. "Then, who are the suspects in this case?"

"What about Clyde Pochard?" someone said. "Everyone here saw him on the beach earlier. It would be to his advantage to take the stone so he could buy the land."

This **enraged** the leaders of the two villages.

"Don't point your wing tip at me," said the leader of Kawai's village.

"This robbery would never

have happened if *they* weren't so anxious to sell the land," said the leader of Kai's village.

"How do we know that *you* didn't take it yourself for some greedy reason?" the other leader yelled.

Kai and Kawai looked at each other and shook their heads as if to say, "It's no use. The feuding has started all over again."

Miss Mallard spoke up and said, "Quarreling will not help us solve this case. Any one of you could have taken the stone."

"You mean we're all suspects?" asked the two village leaders.

"For certain, until this case is solved," replied Miss Mallard. "Many of you were hopping up and down to fetch things during the feast, so you have weak **alibis.**

"I suggest," she continued cooly, "that we all retire for the night. I'll give this case some thought and **resume** this investigation in the morning."

"Kawai and I will walk back to your inn with you, Miss Mallard," said Kai.

Miss Mallard packed her tools and the key chain in her knitting bag while Kai and Kawai lit a lantern. Then they left together on a path through the jungle. It was a shortcut to Miss Mallard's inn.

4

On the Run!

The night was pitch-black, and a brisk wind whistled through the palm **fronds**. But as the three walked, they heard another sound and looked behind them. It was the sound of leaves and branches

being crushed by footsteps. **They were being followed!**

"Run!" said Kai to Kawai and Miss Mallard.

They ran as fast as they could and finally reached the inn. They had escaped their **pursuer**.

"Who was following us?" asked Miss Mallard, quite out of breath.

"I don't know," said Kai, "but we are not going back to find out. Kawai and I will take the long way home along the beach."

"Let me call a driver," said Miss

Mallard. "I would feel much better if someone here drove you home."

She arranged at the inn for a driver to take them home in a jeep. She stood on the front porch and watched them ride away.

Then, just before she turned to go inside, she shivered. She felt like there was someone **lurking** in the jungle, watching her. And waiting. She opened the door and ran to the safety of her room.

Miss Mallard made some notes about the case in her notebook.

She wrote down all the possible **motives** for the crime. Then she stared for a long time at the key chain.

Finally, she put away her notes and the key chain and got ready for bed. She climbed under the covers and turned off the light.

But she had trouble sleeping. She tossed and turned all night. And when she did sleep, she dreamed that a scary face was chasing her!

5

Special Delivery

When morning finally came, Miss Mallard had a plan. She put on a **bulky** sweater, a cap, and dark glasses to disguise herself as a delivery person. Then she wrapped the key chain in a box

and tied the box with a ribbon.

She was certain that the carved scary face belonged to one of the three suspects.

But which suspect?

"Now for my first delivery," she said as she left the inn.

Miss Mallard's first stop was at the home of Clyde Pochard, her first suspect. She rang the bell at Pochard's front door. Pochard himself opened it.

"I have a delivery here for you from Norman's Department

Store," said Miss Mallard in a disguised voice.

"I didn't order anything from there," said Pochard.

Miss Mallard insisted that he open the box to see if he had placed the order. Pochard opened the box and took out the carved scary face.

"I would never order this silly key chain," he said angrily. **"Take it back! I've never seen it before."**

Pochard slammed the door.

42

"What a shame," thought Miss Mallard. "I hoped the key chain might be for his bulldozer."

Miss Mallard's next stop was at Horace Shoveller's digging site.

Luckily, as she walked along the beach to the digging site, no one recognized her.

"I can't wait to get this itchy sweater off," she thought as she pushed and pulled at it.

Horace Shoveller was at work digging as she approached him.

"Excuse me, sir. I have brought

this for you from Makani's Antique Shop," said Miss Mallard.

"For me?" said Horace Shoveller. "I wonder what it could be."

He opened the box, and his beak dropped.

"What *is* this ugly thing?" he cried. "**A key chain?** *Really!* This is not for me."

He tossed the box back to Miss Mallard.

"I'm sorry about the mistake," said Miss Mallard. "Perhaps the store thought the carving of the

scary face would interest you."

"Never!" Horace Shoveller shouted angrily. "I only collect rare art. Take it back."

As Miss Mallard went on her way, she thought, "That clears the second suspect."

Miss Mallard's last stop was at Joe Scaup's shack on the **wharf.** She found him packing a rowboat.

"Are you going somewhere?" asked Miss Mallard.

"That's none of your business!" said Joe Scaup.

"Well, I have a package for you from Sadie's Curio Shop," said Miss Mallard.

"What are you talking about?" said Joe Scaup. "I've never heard of Sadie's Curio Shop."

6

The Jig Is Up!

Miss Mallard insisted that he open the box. Joe Scaup opened the lid and looked inside.

He saw the key chain and gasped!

Miss Mallard knew at once that

the key chain was Joe Scaup's.

"Where did you get this?" he yelled. "Who sent you?"

"So it was *you* who took the stone!" said Miss Mallard as she ripped off her dark glasses.

"Great Davy Jones's locker!" shouted Joe Scaup. "Miss Mallard herself! How did you know I took it?"

Miss Mallard replied, "I knew you did it when I saw the face carved from a shark's tooth. It is a sailor's hobby to make carvings

like this. But just like all good ducktectives, I wanted to be sure, so I checked out the other suspects first."

Miss Mallard continued, "I knew the key chain didn't belong to any of the villagers because they live in grass huts and don't need keys. You had better return the stone and forget your plan to run away with the goods.

"Where is that stone?" she demanded.

"It's in my canvas bag," said

Joe Scaup. "I should have known you would find me out!

"That's why I chased you in the jungle when I remembered the key chain," he added. "I wanted to get it back from you. But you were too quick for me."

"So it *was* you in the jungle last night," said Miss Mallard. "But why did you take the stone?"

"I know plenty of people who would buy it from me," said Joe Scaup. "I could have made myself some real money and . . .

I CAN STILL DO IT!" he proclaimed.

He grabbed a rope and **hurled** himself at Miss Mallard.

"I'm going to leave you tied up in my shack while I row away with the stone to another island," he said.

"I was ready for this," said Miss Mallard, quickly leaping out of the way.

In a flash she reached into her knitting bag and pulled out the conch shell she had found.

Miss Mallard held it up as she had seen Kai do on the beach.

"Aaaawoooooooo!" She blew into the shell hard.

"Cut that out!" cried Joe Scaup.

He was too late. Everyone came running from all over and headed directly for the wharf. Even the police came this time. Kai and Kawai were the first to get there.

"I've discovered the stone," said Miss Mallard. "It's in Joe's Scaup's canvas bag."

Kai and Kawai opened the bag, and sure enough, the stone was there. Miss Mallard told the police everything, and Joe Scaup was taken away to jail.

As everyone left to replace the stone on the pedestal, Clyde Pochard came tearing along in his bulldozer.

This time he narrowly missed hitting a policeman and was given a ticket.

And another ticket for driving on the beach. And still another

for putting everyone's lives in **jeopardy**.

"That's a lot of tickets," said Kai to Miss Mallard. "It will be a relief not to see him and his bulldozer on the beach."

"And one less risk for me when I go surfing," said Miss Mallard.

"Which reminds me," said Kawai, **"SURF'S UP!"**

The three of them ran to get their surfboards.

"Oh my," said Miss Mallard, looking at the surf. "I've never ridden waves that big before."

"You can do it, Miss Mallard," said Kai and Kawai together. **"You can do anything!"**

And so the three of them jumped into the water on their surfboards and paddled out to sea.

Word List

alibis (AL·li·byes): Excuses or reasons given for not being guilty

bulky (BUL·key): Large and thick

conch (KHANCH): A type of seashell

enraged (en·RAYGD): Made very angry

feud (FEWD): A fight that lasts a long time

fronds (FRAHNDS): Long, large leaves

hula (WHO·lah): A traditional Hawaiian dance

hurled (HERLD): Threw with force

jeopardy (JEP·ar·dee): Danger or harm

luau (LOO·ow): A Hawaiian feast

lurking (LUR·king): Hiding

motives (MO·tivs): Reasons for doing something

poi (POY): A Hawaiian food made from a mashed plant

pursuer (pur·SOO·er): A person who chases or follows someone

resume (ree·ZOOM): Begin again after stopping

tidal wave (TIE·dahl wayv): An unusually high sea wave

unison (YOO·nih·sun): Together or at the same time

wharf (WORF): A structure built along a seashore where boats dock

Questions

1. Do you think it would be hard or easy for Miss Mallard to learn to surf? What would make it easy? What would make it hard?

2. What were the two families fighting about?

3. After Miss Mallard discovered that the stone was missing, what was the first clue she found?

4. What disguise did Miss Mallard choose for herself? What did she wear?

5. What was the reason the thief took the stone?

Acknowledgments

My thanks and appreciation go to Jon Anderson, president and publisher of Simon & Schuster Children's Books, and his talented team: Karen Nagel, executive editor; Karin Paprocki, art director; Tiara Iandiorio, designer; Elizabeth Mims, managing editor; Sara Berko, production manager; Tricia Lin, assistant editor; and Richard Ackoon, executive coordinator; for launching out into the world again these incredible new editions of my Miss Mallard Mystery books for today's young readers everywhere.